Skye's
Social Situation

Written by
**Nicole
Natale**

Illustrated by
**Jasmine
Bailey**

Vocabulary

Social Media............ websites and applications that let users create and share content.

Digital .... information stored on computers, phones, and other devices.

Cairngorm Mountains... the only free range herd of reindeer in the United
Reindeer Preserve — Kingdom, located in the Cairngorm Mountains in Scotland.

Nessie.................. The mythical creature from the freshwater lake Loch Ness. Also known as the Loch Ness monster.

Preserve............... A place to maintain a habitat or to protect animals.

Scottish words - English translation:

Buannaiche.... winner

Cuthach........ mad

Halo .... hello

Laddie......... younger boy

Loch .... lake

Pure Barry .... wonderful

Rìoghail........ royal

Sona........... happy

Trang.......... busy

**For Chris, Noël, Nicholas, Cookie, and Ike,
who inspire and delight me daily.**

Copyright © 2021 by Joy Holiday Publishing LLC

Book design by the Virtual Paintbrush.

ISBN 978-1-956146-03-5

It's summer vacation in the North Pole. The lead reindeer sleigh puller, Skye, has one last stop before heading home to Scotland for a visit...Hawaii! She needs to drop off Santa and his family for their vacation.

Home! She sees the Cairngorm Mountains where she is from in Scotland and the reindeer preserve where she grew up. There is her herd! She's so excited to be with her family and **blether** (have a good chat).

Her little family clan greets her with a **"halo"** (hello). Kenzy, her mother; Bruce, her father; Sandy, her grandfather; Gair, her brother; Bonnie and Aileana, her reindeer friends; and Tom, the caretaker of the reindeer preserve, are all there. Gair, who's a little **laddie** (younger boy), cheers, "Skye's home!"

Skye's visit is just in time for the last day of the Reindeer Games. Reindeer compete in all of the skills needed in the North Pole, like speed, strength, flying, finding their way through mazes, and solving puzzles. Gair, Bonnie, and Aileana compete, along with reindeer from different clans. Bonnie is the fastest in the sprint, the most important skill to get a sleigh into the sky.

Aileana watches confident Bonnie carry her heavy present sack to victory. She's the **buannaiche** (winner).

Bonnie wins the grand prize of the Reindeer Games. Gair excitedly proclaims, "I win, I win!" as he gets a participation prize. He's so excited that his sister can share in the moment. She's not around as much as he'd like. Skye's **Sona** (happy) she's there, too. "Congratulations Gair, amazing game play!"

All the reindeer sing and dance together while watching the celebration fireworks:

O where and O where does your highland laddie dwell;

O where and O where does your highland laddie dwell;

He dwells in merry Scotland where the bluebells sweetly smell,

And all in my heart I love my laddie well.

"It was so much fun watching you compete! It was **pure barry** (wonderful). You're both so athletic!" says Skye. "Why don't we all go running by the Loch and visit Nessie tomorrow?"

Aileana and Bonnie are excited. "Yes!" they say together.

Grandpa Sandy, Bruce, Kenzy, and Gair are ready for their celebration dinner of carrots, apples, green moss, mushrooms, bark, and berries. Skye's mom Kenzy says, "I'm so happy my little girl will be back at the table for dinner!"

It's been so long since Skye has been home," Grandpa Sandy complains. Tom the caretaker has some pages from online social media to share with the reindeer family. "North Pole Elfie has posted some great pictures of Skye," Kenzy says, "That's how I get most of my news about my little girl."

Skye laughs and reminds her mom, "You can't always believe what Elfie posts. I'm **trang** (busy) mostly doing hard work for Santa."

Gair asks Skye,"Wanna see my room?" Skye is shocked to see all of the social media posts printed out and on Gair's wall. "I'm so embarrassed. I didn't know Elfie was posting so much about me." Gair replied, "Well, I'm glad. I miss you. Without those posts, I'd never see you."

The next morning, Skye, Bonnie, and Aileana visit the shores of **Loch Ness** (Lake Ness). Skye is having so much fun, she says, "We should camp overnight!"

Skye suggests, "Let's hike to the abandoned castle and stay there." Bonnie remarks, "Of course you want to stay in the castle. You must be used to the **rìoghail** (royal) life in the North Pole." Aileana echoes this, "I understand why you never want to come home and visit the herd. It must be so wonderful being part of Santa's reindeer team." Skye doesn't know what to say.

Nessie pops up to say hi. Skye talks to her alone. "Why does everyone think I don't want to come home or that all I do is have fun?" Nessie answers, "I guess they only know what they see, and they don't see you here very often."

It's Skye's dad Bruce's birthday, which is the main reason Skye has come home to the herd. "Dad, I brought you some tropical fruit from Hawaii and a special ornament made by Mrs. Claus."

Their little family herd celebrates Bruce's birthday under the twinkling stars, happy they're all together for dad's special day.

The next day, Skye goes to see Tom. "Skye, I'm so glad you've offered to help work in the stable today," Tom says. Skye spends the day moving items and training smaller reindeer on sleigh-pulling techniques.

Gair follows Skye as she does more volunteer work. She visits another local preserve and plays with wild Konik ponies. "Look Gair, we can also visit with the Whooper swans, pink-footed geese, terns, and sparrows. Let's see if they're hungry. Every June 25th during summer vacation my North Pole friends Lizzy and Mike share how they've helped our animal friends. I'm so glad we have something to share, too!"

"Is this the kind of work you do with Santa?" Gair asks. Skye answers, "I'm sorry I haven't taken more time to share with you what I'm up to when I'm not here. Santa has a pretty good mail system. I'm going to make you my pen pal from now on."

Skye and Gair take down the social posts and put up a picture of them together.
"Skye, I want to know the good stuff and the bad stuff when you write me letters, and
I'll do the same!" Gair is happy to have a new plan to keep in touch with his sister.

Skye says, "Well, I'm all packed up. I've got to get back to work and pick up Santa and his family in Hawaii." Aileana has packed her own bag. "I'm going to come and help out for a bit. I'm ready for a little adventure." Skye warns Aileana, "It's hard work, but you're welcome to come."

"What about you Bonnie?" Aileana asks. Bonnie replies, "I've seen all I need to see of the North Pole from Elfie's posts. Not interested." Skye says, "Please don't be **cuthach** (mad) Bonnie. I'm sorry for not keeping in touch more. I promise to do better."

"Make sure you write!" calls Gair. "Spend more time working and less time playing," calls out Grandpa. "You can come anytime, not just for birthdays," Bruce comments. "Eat more carrots and less candy! I see all of those sweets that Elfie posts," Kenzy scolds.

"I'll write and come home more! Don't believe everything you see online, Grandpa!
Mom, I'll eat some fruit as soon as I get to Hawaii."

Aileana has her first job, and it's an important one: She's helping to bring Santa and his family home from vacation! "Aileana, make sure you fly steady. Titina doesn't like a bumpy ride. She's a very particular pup!" says Skye.

After a long day of work, Aileana says, "This isn't as fun as I thought it would be. When do we play?" "Not until the weekend," Skye reminds Aileana.

"Hey, Aileana. How do you like the North Pole?" Elfie wonders. "Well, it doesn't seem much like your posts," she responds. Elfie laughs. "I only post happy, fun stuff. I don't think anyone wants to know about my bad days."

Aileana is ready to go back to Scotland. She takes a picture before she goes. "Say cheese! One photo for everyone back at the herd in Scotland."

When she gets home, Aileana talks to the herd about the picture and Skye. "It was a lot of hard work, and Skye really misses home. I guess we can't believe everything we see online." Bonnie is happy that her old friend Skye will be back in their lives and not just a distant online post.

BY DOING SIMPLE ACTS OF KINDNESS,
we can't help
BUT LIFT OURSELVES UP, TOO

Tips on staying connected online and offline:

- Write letters, postcards, or even just a Post-It note in an envelope and drop them in a mailbox.

- Make sure to share the good and the bad.

- Send a personalized text, photo, or voice message.

- Call someone on the phone.

Whatever you do, make a personal connection with your loved ones. Don't count on social media to tell your story. It's fun to see pictures of family and friends on social media, but the stories behind those pictures are often more interesting, and you can only get those from the people themselves.

Scottish Fruit Bread

Yield: 2 Loaves

Ingredients
¾ cup AP flour or (gluten-free Cup4Cup Flour)
1 tsp Baking soda
1 tsp Baking powder
1 tsp Salt
¾ cup Light brown sugar
1 cup Apricots, dried, cut into quarters
2 cups Assorted dried fruits (raisins, peaches, pears, apples), diced finely
1 cup Chocolate chips
3 Eggs, beaten
1 tsp Vanilla extract
1 tsp Orange extract

Directions
1. Preheat the oven to 325 degrees F. Grease two 8.5 X 4.5 X 2.5 inch loaf pans. Don't forget to grease the sides as well. Set aside until ready to fill.
2. Whisk the flour, baking soda, baking powder, and salt together in a large mixing bowl.
3. Add the brown sugar, breaking up any large clumps. Add in all the dried fruit and chocolate chips and stir well with a spatula to coat with dry ingredients.
4. In a small bowl, beat the eggs with both extracts. Add into the fruit mixture, and stir until fully incorporated.
5. Divide the mix evenly between both loaf pans and place on a lower shelf in the oven. The bread will rise while baking. Bake for 40 minutes total, rotating pans 180 degrees halfway through baking time. When done, the bread should look golden brown on top, edges coming away from the loaf pan, and a toothpick or knife inserted in the center of the loaf should come out clean. Slice and enjoy while warm.

Optional Add-Ins
Omit ½ cup of apricots and add in ½ cup sunflower seeds or ½ cup toasted coconut flakes.
Omit chocolate chips and add in white chocolate chips or butterscotch chips.
Omit orange extract and add in your favorite extract.

Lightning Source UK Ltd.
Milton Keynes UK
UKHW050815090223
416624UK00003B/206